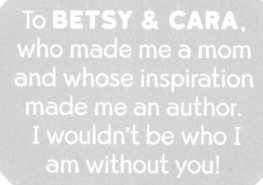

To **BETSY & CARA**, who made me a mom and whose inspiration made me an author. I wouldn't be who I am without you!

978-1-7374325-0-0

the MONSTER TREATY of in·betweeny

written by KP Loundy

illustrated by Lucy Shin

Some time ago there was a sad situation,
better described as a

MONSTER
frustration.

No one knew where they came from,
or where all they went,
but they were not liked
100 percent.

They sometimes were **LARGE**, or **furry**, or small,

but they seemed to bother kids most of all.

They'd peek from the CLOSETS,
the **CURTAINS,**
and **CHAIRS**
startling children
with their monstery stares.

Always appearing where they were least wanted,
shrieks and cries left the monsters undaunted.

Children were frightened,
and parents were vexed.
They never could tell
where a scare would be next.

Until two brave parents said,
"THAT IS ENOUGH!
IT'S TIME TO GET SMART
IT'S TIME TO GET TOUGH."
Their sweet little daughter was no longer sleeping,
so worried was she about all of the peeping.

Others had tried
to trap them and failed.
They couldn't be captured,

BUT COULD
THEY BE
TAILED?

"They're too quick to catch, but there may be a chance
to stop them from popping up in advance."

They hopped into bed, with the covers pulled tight,
then pretended to sleep as they spied in the night.

Until what was that?
Two bright monster eyes!
They threw back the covers
and shouted,

SURPRISE!

The monster squeaked
and took off like a bandit,
revealing his path
just like they had planned it.

Instead of a closet
they found a new world,

where all around

COLORS and
puffs of stuff
swirled.

They sped around corners and slipped through the cracks,
skipping through shadows of greys and blacks.

They ran and they ran
til their feet were quite sore,
and though they felt tired
they kept running some more.
With only a glimpse
or a footprint to track,
both parents were worried
but wouldn't turn back.

They finally stopped
at a door
in·between,
The monster they followed?
Nowhere to be seen.

When they opened the door just a bit not too wide,
what greeted them was a lush countryside.

They expected their home to be
gloomy and **dreary**,
but the land that they saw
was really quite

CHEERY.

Mom and Dad stood in awe. They were simply astounded!
Too late they realized, they were wholly surrounded.
One monster was plenty! This many were scary.
The monsters as well seemed especially wary.

The silence was so loud you could hear a dropped pin,
the quiet dragged on with no sight of an end.
They both were afraid what the other may do,
so they stayed still until someone sneezed,

"ACHOO!!"

One monster **giggled**
and another **GUFFAWED**,
all their cold feelings
were thoroughly thawed.

Mom quickly said
"BLESS YOU",
and Dad had a tissue,
and suddenly there
was no longer an issue.

The monster was grateful,
and blew quite discreetly,
then gave a big smile and
thanked them both sweetly.

Everyone saw
that the others were nice.
That well-timed **sneeze**
had broken the ice.

They explained to the monsters that they caused such a fright,
when spied in the dark by children at night.
And the monsters were all very sorry and sad,
because even a monster knows scaring is bad.
Their goal wasn't to scare, they just wanted a peek.
But monsters aren't very good at hide and go seek.
All of the reactions they viewed all the same,
the cries and the jumps just a part of the game.

Monsters were no good at hiding and too good at seeking,
clearly their rules would need some more tweaking.
The parents asked, "Well do you have a suggestion,
how we may handle our children's objection?'

So the monsters decided it would be best for all,
if they created a new monster law.

No monster would settle in any dark places,
in order to catch a quick glimpse of kids' faces.

They wrote it all down feeling very official,
and showed the two parents right where to initial.

The monsters each signed with their name or their mark.
They agreed to no hiding in dimness and dark.

The law was displayed on the door
in·between,
ensuring that it would not go unseen.

Mom and dad returned heroes,
and kids were well rested;
the monsters abided
by all rules requested.

No monsters were lurking
in closets or curtains
The monsters were gone,

of that they were
CERTAIN!

And since that day no monsters have crept,
on slumbering children, in bed as they slept.

THE END.

CPSIA information can be obtained
at www.ICGtesting.com
Printed in the USA
LVHW071040011221
704960LV00006BA/32